Slave: Fulfilling a Prophecy

Rowan Knight

Published by 22 Lions Bookstore, 2019.

Title Page

Slave: Fulfilling a Prophecy
By Rowan Knight

Published by 22 Lions Bookstore and Publishing House

About the Publisher

About the 22 Lions Bookstore:
www.22Lions.com
Facebook.com/22Lions
Twitter.com/22lionsbookshop
Instagram.com/22lionsbookshop
Pinterest.com/22lionsbookshop

Introduction

This book describes a slave's journey from the deepest state of poverty to the fulfillment of a prophecy, a destiny that he himself foresees when he states in his thoughts: "I feel peaceful when I look at the sky, as if I am being embraced in the tranquility of the universe."

How does he respond to the temptations set in his path and all the challenges? With humility and faith in the many strangers he encounters who guide him to his unpredictable end.

Chapter 1 - Despised

I don't remember how my childhood went. All I remember is always feeling hunger, cold and sadness.

Today the sun rises and sets, but I don't feel the days go by. I feel that it is always night, that day runs fast and that there is no hope or meaning in living.

However, I look around and see a crowd eager to devour itself. All that hangs in this society seems to be hate, violence and sex.

Prostitutes abound and this is ironic for marriages that continue to be consummated as a rule.

It seems that wars serve as an excuse for when sex becomes boring. It is an age of violence and suffering in which we live. And yet, humans don't seem to feel their souls, they don't seem to feel the need for purpose in life.

I am poor and so is my family. I live in a corner of a square where every day they look at me like I'm not entitled to a heart that beats and asks for food.

My mother begs every day. Asks for my sisters. For to her I am the devil's son.

She does not consider me her son and brings me with her fundamentally for protection. I'm the man in the family after my father left us.

I know little about him except that he beat me more than my mother. I remember the many days my head bled and my tears streamed down my cheeks and spilled into my chest.

I believe I got used to suffering. And behold, I suddenly wake up from these thoughts. My mother walks toward me.

— "What are you doing, miserable?" she asks, then continuing: — "Are you sitting here? Saying nothing and doing nothing? You are a worm. You make me sick!", And ending these statements spits on my feet. But soon after turning her back, she regrets, turns back, takes me by the arm, and with an aggressive tug sends me into the crowd and shouts, "Work! I do not deserve you. Monster!"

I look at my twin sisters and think about them, Auria and Nuria. I would like them to love me as my mother does not, but they follow her example in the scorn and contemptuous glances they give me. And after that, I begin by begging among the people who walk in the square.

Many push me, and give me bumps.

As day falls, it is not much I gather. My mother was friendly in giving me some of the bread she could buy with alms. But then she says:

— "If you didn't exist, my life would be easier."

I know so, and shyly answer her:

— "I don't want bread anymore. Give it to my sisters.", But she doesn't answer me.

I turn away to what feeds my spirit and deceives my stomach, which is looking at the stars. I feel peaceful when I look at the sky, as if I am being embraced in the tranquility of the universe.

Chapter 2 - Secrets of the Night

The night goes on and everyone already sleeps.

I take the opportunity to walk a little. And in the meantime I approach the castle to listen to the conversations of the surveillance soldiers.

Sometimes some important philosophers, coming or going to banquets, approach them to talk.

I hear some of the conversations. And today it seems that one of Nephrates' disciples tells a joke about his master. Everyone laughs!

I approach the brambles and bushes to hear better without being seen. The disciple continues:

— "My master, however, defends a great truth. He believes that the universe was built by humans but everyone forgot about it. Our souls are intoxicated by the lust of the flesh and are therefore disconnected from the great universal truth that we are all children of the gods, and worthy of their powers. But I said to him, "Master, don't you enjoy sex with your handmaid? Or when she spreads her legs, are you looking for universal knowledge?"

Everyone laughed a lot. And the disciple goes on:

— "My master was so drunk he looked at me and said, "Don't question the truth of the gods because they will punish you, and... and... and...", And he fell round to the ground. Some of those at the banquet laughed even more when they saw him fall and roll like a skewer pig. Ahahah "

The soldiers and the disciple couldn't stop laughing so hard.

Meanwhile, I neglected myself and made a noise by stepping on a dry stick.

They hear, look around, but see nothing.

— "Anybody here? Show yourself!", Asks one of the soldiers.

I keep crouching and in complete silence until they ignore me.

The soldier picks up a rock and throws it towards me, striking me in the left arm. But I remain still, and without making any noise.

Fearing for his reputation, and that anyone would hear the story, the philosopher's disciple decides to end his conversation by saying goodbye to the soldiers.

Shortly after I fall asleep.

Chapter 3 - Visits in the Kingdom

I wake up the next day to the noise of the wagons.

I stride to the center of the village where I realize that everyone seems to be carefully groomed, although we always wear the same rags.

I ask what is going on and they tell me that a great king is coming to our land.

Hulu Inis is his name. He comes from India to trade with the Turkey-based Roman general.

My mother runs with my sisters to kneel by the caravan. It is a custom for our entire population to do so.

There is no particular obligation in this. We just fear that someone will notice us and take it as an insult.

Nobles tend to have the humblers killed for the sake of pure amusement whenever they feel them undermining their reputation.

Going down, if necessary, with our faces on the floor, saves us a lot of embarrassment and serious problems, and allows us to maintain life.

I remember one of my friends being executed simply for daring to look a king in the eye. One of his generals made sure to take a sword and, thrusting it into his limbs several times, left him to bleed at the gates of the holy temple, now owned by the Roman army.

As the entourage passes, my mother notices that they come to buy slaves.

Our nation refused to fight, and what it did not pay for dead soldiers eventually paid for the delivery of slaves and tithes.

We are a broken and poor nation monetarily and spiritually. But the pride of many prevails and they refuse to accept it. Not even our king accepts it. And so it is with a big hypocritical smile that he shows them a huge line of our most beautiful women and our strongest men.

My mother also notes that with the king come several women. Possibly maids or concubines, or even both.

— "Look how beautiful they are, and what angel dresses they bring with them!" My mother notes, addressing my sisters.

Among them, the princess, his daughter, discreet and hidden behind royal robes that hide her face, is inside one of the chariots that brings them here.

I see many soldiers and escorts of dark skin, mixed, white and other colors I can't quite describe.

It is somewhat difficult to distinguish each other's functions too, as they do not seem to occupy predefined positions that we are used to seeing. There are women soldiers, of imposing size and the appearance of those who have the strength of a thousand bulls, and there are also young women among the king's helpers.

They seem to surround the king all the time, helping him with his garments and objects. Some closer to him share much information and thoughts.

The princess is still in her wagon, discreetly looking through the curtains. It seems to me that she looked at me, but I am probably wrong. There are many people around me.

Chapter 4 - Betrayed

My mother turns away from me and my sisters. I do not know why. But I stand next to them, quiet and serene.

They are still very young, and I have to protect them, even if I am not strong enough to fight like a soldier.

My mother goes to talk to one of the senior soldiers. And the soldier looks at me suspiciously.

I do not know what's happening. But shortly after she comes to me.

— "Go to that gentleman. He has something for you."

I obey her, confused, and approach this general.

— "Come with me!", He calmly and succinctly says.

I follow him, watching my mother indignantly, who doesn't seem to want to look at me anymore.

She seems absorbed between feelings of sadness and tranquility.

However, in a sudden gesture, the general takes me by the neck and calls some men in a language I do not know.

They run fast toward me, and soon after strip my clothes off my body.

Startled, tears stream down my cheeks, for I don't know what my destiny is.

— "What harm did I do to deserve to be punished?", I ask them with tremendous anxiety. But they do not respond, and I continue: — "Forgive me for listening to the philosopher's conversations. I won't do that again."

They keep ignoring my words, as if they were unrelated to their intentions. And then I insist: — "Please let me go! I did nothing to you! Please, gentlemen, let me go!"

Now completely naked, they walk away as a strong woman, soldier like them, but of a higher state, approaches me, puts her hand on my chest, and looks at me with lust as she smiles.

She says something I don't understand.

However, very close to my body, she touches me everywhere, as if investigating and examining my physical condition. And then she gets even closer to sniff my neck.

At this point, her right hand touches my chest again, and goes down to my abdomen, continuing towards my genitals. She grips them tightly in her hand and kisses me as she holds them.

Her tongue seems to continue to analyze me, controlling and testing my potential.

After that, she asks for a blanket to cover me and walks away.

Other men come from behind and hurriedly bind my wrists with chains. And I don't know what that kiss brought with it, because I feel myself fainting with dizziness. Maybe she gave me some drugs to calm me down.

I am afraid, not knowing if they will kill me or use me to be eaten by some animal for the amusement of the masses.

They pull me into the center of the crowd, and I find my mother, who sees me once again. I want to ask her for help but she seems to know what's going on and ignore me. And then, I see a soldier handing her a sack full of coins.

She cries and turns away, disappearing into the crowd.

My sisters keep looking sad at me for a few more seconds, but soon follow her.

I could read in their eyes that this was a farewell and I would not see them again.

I am placed in the slave line to be seen by the king and his maids.

Realizing what is happening, I wipe my tears from my face and surrender my life to the hands of the eternal God and his lucky messengers.

Chapter 5 - Chosen

I notice that I am still very young and weak compared to the other men and women offered as slaves.

I have lived so many days of hunger that I think my body has also taken on a shape of its own because I am thin, very slight, and with big sad eyes, always in a subservient posture.

Even the other slaves seem to be able to remain more straight than me.

However, the choices begin.

There are about twenty-seven among us to be offered to the king. I am the twenty-eighth. But the king says he wants only six.

In the end, the king stops for a few seconds, and looks at me without saying a word.

He seems puzzled while watching me with a suspicious look, as if I'm very different from the others.

Pointing at me, others realize that I would be the seventh in that choice.

I'm placed in a row with the others, and then taken to the last row of the caravan. We wait there, until late, as everyone heads for a large banquet.

Chapter 6 - The Message

Night falls, but hunger and thirst are always quenched by the king's maids. One of them has mercy on me and while I drink shyly but with great thirst she caresses my head and looks at me with compassion. Her right hand holds the bowl of water and her left hand rests on my head, gently descending to my cheek where it stops as I finish drinking.

It was one of the most loving gestures I felt until that day. I had never felt anything like this. It was very comforting. It even seemed like she was falling in love with me.

— "Hope to see you soon," She said, almost whispering in my ear when I was done, then shyly walking away from me.

As she continued to feed the remaining slaves who were with me, I searched for some friends, but could not see anyone whom I could recognize. And then I leaned against the rock beside me to sleep.

It is common for the dead to talk to me during my dreams, and again this happened.

I never feel fear, but rather tranquility when this happens. It's like they want to help me.

Through these dreams, several people from my village who had already passed away approach me and touch me amicably. Some even kneel in front of me. But I can't always understand what they say. They speak a dialect I don't know.

It seems to me that they want to say something repeatedly, but I can't quite understand what it is.

However, one of them, taller and dressed in black, approaches, and the others move away at the same time. He grabs me with his right hand in my right hand and says:

— "Your old days are over and new days will come. Take it easy, for you are not a child of this world and we are with you all the time so that you do not feel alone in this spiritual journey. By day, as by night, we are by your side", He said.

— "Who am I?" I ask.

— "You are the only one who is. And we are to you as you are to us," He replies, soon after turning away with the other spirits.

A large image of deep white invades my mind, as if flooding with an energy of light, peace and tranquility.

I awake the next day, and hastily, with the kicking of one of the soldiers, telling us that we were about to start a great trip.

— "Come on, come on, quick! I want everyone up and lining up," The soldier told the group.

Chapter 7 - The Journey

I hear the horns play. The sun has risen and the nobles are waking up for the journey ahead.

The camels rise together with the king's men. And he, along with the princess beside him, heads toward the caravan.

After the farewells and other formalities, we set out on our way.

As I left my land, I expected to see someone I knew. At the very least, my own family. But no one was there to say goodbye to me.

My heart is in a great grasp, such is the suffering felt. But I respect the destinies God places on my path, and in reverence and humility I follow with the caravan. Sadness consumes me but I can't stop.

Some time later, the princess puts her head out the window, and looks back, placing me in the landscape of her beautiful eyes. Somehow she seems to empathize with me. But I dare not look her in the face.

I am not worthy of such honors. I lower my eyes and head toward the ground as I walk.

As we leave the desert sands, the ground changes and becomes harder to walk. Some of my fellow travelers complain about their wounds. And the king gives orders to camp on the spot.

As we stop, we notice how beautiful this place is.

It's still daytime. The sun's rays pass through the leaves of the trees.

Suddenly, the princess notices that I am looking toward a large white-winged bird and she looks too, indignant with me. But I'm interrupted with a tap on the shoulder.

— "Go find firewood with these soldiers who will help you," they tell me.

I have to help prepare the dinner of the king's subjects.

As I prepare for the walk, I hear the princess asking to join my group to get to know the region.

The king allows and orders five more guards to accompany the princess.

As we walk, I realize that the place looks very calm. I have never seen anything like it. It is a tranquility that has nothing to do with the daily noise of the village where I lived with my sisters. And what are they doing now? Are they all right? I was thinking to myself. I believe the great God of the planet protects them.

— "Ahhhh, my head!" I shout.

— "Are you ok?" Asks the princess in the distance.

— "I felt a strong pain! I apologize for shouting your highness.", I answered.

It was as if this pain was some kind of warning to leave that place. But a soldier soon interrupts:

— "Hurry up because we don't have all day," And he gets ready to take the whip out of his belt. But the princess soon stops him by placing her delicate hand over his.

— "It is not necessary," She says. And walks towards me: — "Let me help you!"

— "I cannot allow it, your highness."

— "Come on, don't worry. It's fun for me to look for firewood with you."

At this point, I notice something strange among the animals. I look up and notice the birds flying away.

One of the soldiers also seems to feel that something strange is happening and unwraps his sword, while the others simply look at us strangely.

Chapter 8 - The Shadows

Suddenly, something like an arrow crosses the neck of one of the soldiers. But we just heard a thin sound coming from the air. Nobody saw the arrow or the attacker.

His neck begins to release a splash of blood as the soldier falls to the ground, dead.

The soldier who has his sword raised quickly throws his spear into a bush where we see nothing. But a sharp, harsh scream, annoying to the ears, comes out.

Shadows move quickly toward us. They appear only visible in soil and trees.

We can't see what is coming. And while the other soldiers tremble in fear, I can keep calm, for I hear a voice from the invisible:

— "Fear nothing, but be ready!"

The shadows immediately line up between me and the soldiers and attack them all at once, who are unable to defend themselves, and then surround the princess at once.

She looks calm.

They then they start speaking in a strange and very fast language with her.

I can't understand anything, but it looks like the language of the dead, the same I heard before in my dreams.

Soon after, these beings materialize in black robes and cloaks, and look at me before disappearing into the trees of the forest.

Everyone except one who walks over to me and stares at me, perplexed, before joining the others.

I am interrupted by the princess.

— "Come with me! Don't be afraid!", The princess tells me as she takes my hand.

We head back, like a pair of lovers, for she never leaves my hand. Until we get to the camp, and she takes her hand to scream in a frightened tone.

— "This young man saved me from a tragic death. All the other soldiers protecting us died. But thanks to this slave I am alive."

— "What happened? Who attacked you?", Asks the king.

— "Devils! We have never seen anything like it. They were demons!", Replies the princess in a complete faked fright.

The king approaches me and, placing his hand on my shoulder, says:

— "Very well, my boy! God is with you and protects you thanks to your courage and dedication. Today you will have dinner among nobles!"

— "Thank you, your highness, but I am not worthy of such an offer. Out of respect for everyone, and especially my fellow travelers, I ask you to let me return to the group I belong to," I said shyly.

The king was amazed at my humility.

— "With all due respect, my boy, may your will be served!", And that said, he let me go back to the group.

When I reach the group of slaves, I take my bowl to eat the same as them. And I wonder what really happened.

I can't understand what is happening to the princess, or why she had such conversation with these creatures who murdered her soldiers.

Chapter 9 - Rituals

Night comes, and some retire to pray. A very beautiful young black woman who was among us, and with a religion quite different from the rest of the group, approaches.

— "Do you want to join me to pray?", She asks.

— "How do you pray?" I ask her.

— "My religion is about a practice of union with the universe. The goal is to enter the light field that unites everything."

— "Are you telling me that everything is composed of the same energy?"

— "Yes!", She responds promptly. — "All stones, animals, and plants come together in one universal structure, and the importance of being connected with such a source of energy."

—"This attitude towards life is very interesting. I would like to understand more!", I said while joining her.

We leaned toward the ground for a few seconds in reverence for the lunar goddess, and then sat with our backs straight and our eyes closed.

— "Be calm, and relax, that the goddess communicates with you like that!", She tells me.

She must have realized that I wasn't connected enough to my soul, because she put her left hand on the ground and the right one just below my neck.

— "Relax!" She said again, to reassure me.

At that moment, I feel a huge current of energy running through my body. And I can't understand where such energy begins and ends. I just know it goes through my head and down my spine to my limbs.

My hands and feet seem to burn like fire.

She keeps asking me to be calm:

— "Do not be afraid! The fire you feel is the natural burning of the negative energy in you. Mother nature is purifying you. Stay calm!"

Although it feels as if my whole body is on fire, the moment is extraordinary with this great force in me.

My mind seems to be expanding and breaking free from the bonds of fears. I feel a greater harmony with what is around me, as if with my eyes closed and at this moment I can feel the movements of all people, animals, everything. And then we finish.

— "How do you feel?" She asks. — "By the way, my name is Jingh", She says with a smile.

— "I feel great!", I answer in a very calm and cheerful tone, but also confused. She hugs me.

— "I'm so glad you joined me", And, immediately, Jingh takes a bracelet off her right arm and puts it in my hand.

— "This bracelet represents the force of the earth. You need more than me. I already have many years of practice. This bracelet will help you more now that you are beginning this spiritual journey."

— "Thank you very much!", I answer humbly.

Jingh gives me one more big hug and retreats to join the other servants. And I retire to my place of rest. But I hear a voice that makes me look back.

— "Wait!", Says Jingh as she runs to me.

She then takes my face in her hands and kisses me.

— "Good night!", She says with a smile as she runs back, not letting me answer.

Chapter 10 - A Parallel World

At night, the soldiers are on high alert due to what happened.

Some of the ladies are singing to help the soldiers stay awake.

One even starts dancing around the fire, seductively. She is essentially dancing with herself, expressing her beauty, but the soldiers stare at her, mesmerized, while the rest of the entourage sleep soundly.

Suddenly, I hear a slight squeak from a wagon door as the king snores inside.

It's the princess, leaving carefully and discreetly.

I get up to follow her, curious of what she is going to do, and also to protect her from any danger that may arise.

She moves away far enough and faces the trees.

Her posture is very calm and solid, as if waiting for something, and with complete confidence in herself.

As I lean slightly, and between rocks, I notice her eyes completely white and open, as if possessed by some spirit.

The soldiers don't realize anything. They seem distracted by the ladies.

There are two of them now, dancing around the fire, touching and kissing each other, while a third dances on the ground very sexually.

During such a distraction, the princess begins to speak slowly. But I don't understand what she says and I don't see who she is addressing. There doesn't seem to be anything in front of her.

Someone touches my shoulder and I jump in fright. But quickly put her hand on my mouth. It's Jingh!

— "Don't let them see you. The princess is talking to the Yahzuras. "

— "Who are they?", I ask.

— "Spiritual messengers living between kingdoms; the world of mortals and their world."

— "What world is this?", I ask her.

— "It's the world of the dead!"

I pause in shock.

— "How do they cross into our reality?"

— "In their world there is a portal that connects to ours. But they do not have divine permission to cross it. They have to do it through the living, and this portal always has an opening time limit."

— "I do not understand! Why do they talk to the princess?", I continued asking.

— "She's one of them."

I started to wonder if I was too, because they didn't kill me.

— "What do they want from mortals?"

Suddenly we heard shouts from one of the generals.

— "What are you guys doing? They will kill us all! Get back to work."

It seems that the soldiers gave in to fornication with the dancing maids, because we saw them running with their clothes in hand.

— "Let's go back quickly, before they realize we left the group!", Jingh said as she grabbed my hand and took me with her.

— "Don't look back, because the spirits can feel your presence!", Jingh told me as she hurried me down the safest path.

Already at the camp, I saw the princess arrive in silence.

She stopped and looked toward me, and her eyes turned from white to her normal green. And from her very serious face, she smiled at me, as if she knew I had seen her.

She then got into the royal carriage, and I leaned back to fall asleep.

Chapter 11 — The Arrival at the Palace

In the morning we all woke up to the sound of the trumpet.

I get up and Jingh arrives, takes my arm, and pulls me to her.

— "Are you ok?", She asks.

— "Yes! Why do you ask? "I asked back.

— "You're a brave boy! But do not risk death without a meaning. The Yahzuras are lethal beings, not only in flesh but in spirit. There is a whole world beyond this veil that you do not know. And it's easier that way. In other times..."

— "I don't want talk!" Interrupts a soldier. — "Hurry to walk! We have to get out of here fast!"

I had to separate myself from Jingh so she could go back to her group.

— "I'll tell you later!", She said as she walked away.

Hours later, we were close to the palace and, seeing it, I noticed how beautiful it was.

I had never seen anything like it. It was a paradise between walls. And the hills stretched out in a great green with trees of many colors and fruits, most of which I did not even know existed.

Very close, I realized that the locals were all well dressed, with beautiful clothes of many colors.

They didn't have many adornments, but only a silk cloak over their bodies. For women, this dress was transparent enough to see their naked body. They were practically naked.

— "That's how they get a husband before twenty-five", Jingh whispered in my ear, seeing me astonished by the experience.

On the other hand, men did not look very different from women, as they had long hair and no beard.

Jingh approached me to continue to explain more about that culture.

— "There are no differences between men and women, except in mating rituals. Both dress differently to attract each other in different ways. But other than that, there are women soldiers in the same amount as men, and male and female slaves also interact a lot."

— "Interesting! I've never seen anything like it! ", I replied.

— "Maybe we'll be together!" Jingh said with a mischievous smile, then giving me a slap on the butt.

Chapter 12 - The Unpredictable Royal Palace

We arrived at the palace and were very kindly received. Something very different from the brutality I was used to in my land.

The palace was very clean and tidy inside, with excellent art objects in decoration.

Shortly after, we were separated. But while the other slaves were taken out of the palace, they asked me and Jingh to remain quiet where we were.

In a sign of respect and veneration, and to our surprise, some of the castle maids asked us to follow them, to know our rooms. Jingh was then taken to her room by some ladies, while I was led to another by others.

My room was nice, clean, and quiet, with a window over the valley. And I approached the window in amazement.

— "The view from here is magnificent!", I said with admiration.

But the two ladies did not answer me. Instead they smiled at each other, as if they were happy with my presence.

The door was about to close when they opened it again and told me in my language:

— "I am Kasiah and this is my sister, Zofiah!"

I was very surprised at their level of education and respect, as well as their beauty.

On the other hand, the transparent silk dress they wore made it very difficult for me not to notice the beautiful breasts of these gorgeous sisters.

— "Thank you so much for the kindness you show me!", I said, trying to distract my eyes to their faces and focus on their beautiful eyes.

— "We are princesses and sisters of Yinh who accompanied you on the trip, but if you need anything you can always call us and we will be at your disposal for anything."

I could not understand. The princesses at the disposal of a slave?

— "I should be the one always at your disposal!", I answered humbly, confused by the situation and the tremendous kindness I was receiving.

— "There are many things you will understand later, but for now, you can talk to us as if we were the same", They said smiling, while seeming very happy with my presence.

— "I don't understand!" I blurted out, confused by the situation.

— "You have a good heart and are as we imagined you", Said Zofiah, while looking at Kasiah smiling, who replied:

— "In reality you are much more attractive than I expected."

I didn't know what to answer, but Zofiah continued:

— "Most likely, our father will ask you to accompany him on our activities. But let's show you the palace for now!", And taking my hand, Zofiah pulled me out of the room. But afraid of being punished I stopped her.

— "Please, I am not worthy to touch you."

— "Why, you are not a slave! For now this is all you need to know."

Kasiah could not resist, but approached me without words to kiss me.

— "What are you doing?", Zofiah said as she took her sister away from me. — "It's still too early for this."

And so they were gone, closing the bedroom door while leaving me alone.

— "We'll talk later," Said Zofiah.

The leader of the Yahzuras, Yah-Rah opened his hand toward her, and stopped her in a trance. And within seconds he removed her spirit from the body.

After awakening out of her body, Yah-Rah said to her:

— "You belong to the kingdom of the moon, and there you will be happier."

That said, she saw her body of light disappear.

The king took the opportunity when everyone was distracted to unwrap his sword and place it near Yinh's throat.

— "I will be the only king. There will be no one else in my place. I will not give up everything I have gained from many wars. And I will kill you again if it have to, because if you die, all the Yahzuras lose the reason for the battle and will have to leave", Said the terrified king, while feeling that he had control of the situation at hand.

— "Yes, it is true, my king", Yinh replied him, as she turned to look the king in the eye. — "Except fate does not belong to you. Your time is up."

In saying this, the king felt a tightness in his chest. He was having a heart attack. And he died right there in front of everyone.

— "My people!", Yinh shouted. — "The time has come to fulfill the great prophecy. Among us is a prophet, and the stone of the kingdom of the dead, which I bring in my hand, will reveal who he is. Through him all who have high morality and are empathic will forever be immortalized, and can live between worlds, never forgetting the many previous lives. Our kingdom will consist of immortals."

The villagers, hearing this, understood that the prophecy of the stars was coming true at that time, and they all knelt in front of Yinh in humble veneration.

Chapter 14 - The Prophecy

"I will not be sovereign queen, but queen of my king, together with my sisters, Zofiah and Kasiah. And the three together, we will channel the energy of your king, and prophet. He will be a king between worlds with our help", Yinh said loudly as she extended her hand in front of everyone and opened it so that the stone would undoubtedly reveal who the new king would be.

What looked like a normal black stone became transparent, and then a very bright green light came from the center of this transparency.

The glow of the stone pointed toward me like a ray of light.

Kasiah took my right hand, and Zofiah took my left hand, and they directed me towards Yinh.

— "We knew it was you from the many signals we received, but we needed to wait for the right moment to get confirmation. I'm glad it's really you, because we like you so much", Said Yinh.

At that moment, the Yahzuras disappeared like clouds into the realm of the dead.

From that day on, I occupied the position of king, and with my three queens we formed constant energy rituals that allowed all spirits of good-hearted people to easily reincarnate in our kingdom and to remember all their previous lives.

Thanks to the four of us, and to our kingdom, the energy of the planet was changed. And forever we were the much loved nobles.

Previously a slave, I had become a prophet and king, and forever led the fate of the world with my three beloved queens in the direction of peace, wisdom, harmony, and happiness.

Book Review Request

Dear Reader, Thank you for purchasing this book! I would love to know your opinion. Writing a book review helps in understanding readers and also has an impact on other reader's purchasing decisions. Your opinion matters. Please write a book review! Your kindness is greatly appreciated!

Booklist

Books written by the author:
Agne: Inside the Mind of a Narcissist
Destiny: When Your Soulmate Finds You
Disenchanted: Poems by Rowan Knight
Illusion: When a Nymphomaniac Falls in Love
One Chance: 20 Short Stories with a Plot Twist and Moral Lesson
Prophecy: A Message to Humanity
Slave: Fulfilling a Prophecy
Soulless: Letters to a Narcissist

About the Publisher

This book was published by the 22 Lions Bookstore.
For more books like this visit www.22Lions.com.
Join us on social media at:
Fb.com/22Lions;
Twitter.com/22lionsbookshop;
Instagram.com/22lionsbookshop;
Pinterest.com/22LionsBookshop.